JAM
SUN
CREAM
"Roar, roar, roar!
I'm a little dinosaur.
Sun or snow, off I go!"

Roar is brave
and Roar is strong.
She often likes
to sing a song.

"Pack my bag
with yummy things.
Don't forget
my springy springs."

Roar loves walking
in the rain.
Off she dashes
up the lane.

"I love jumping
in a puddle.
Mud and water,
what a muddle."

Roar sees footprints
big and small,
made by friends
both short and tall.

"Clever beetle,
I've found you.
Worms and crawlies
hiding too!"

Roar likes playing
in the meadow.
Watch her run
and chase her shadow.

"Tickly grass
and buzzy bees.
Swishy swashy
round my knees."

Roar likes dipping
in a pond.
Finding things
from way beyond.

"I love sorting frogs and newts. I wonder if they all play flutes."

Roar, where are you?

Roar loves birds
brown and green.
In the hide
she can't be seen.

“Look at me
counting birds.
Quietly does it,
can’t be heard.”

Roar can climb
the highest mountain.
With her friend,
hear them shouting.

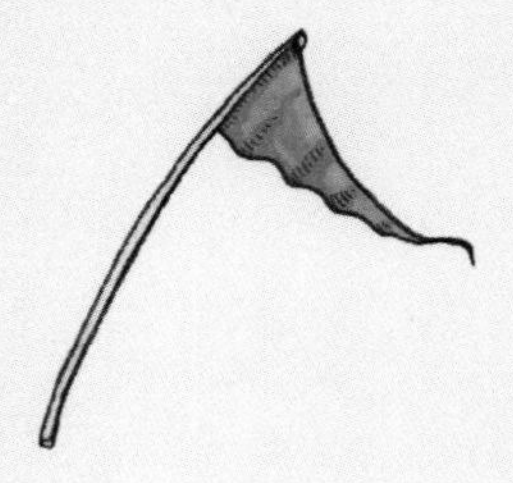

“Up, up, up,
we shall go.
When we get there,
will it snow?”

Roar collects things
at the beach.
Many treasures
she can reach.

"Shells and seaweed,
driftwood too.
Hello, crab,
I like you."

Roar pretends
within a castle.
Dressing up
just like a rascal.

"I'm a princess,
I'm a knight.
I'll jump out,
give you a fright."

Roar loves shower-time,
water falling.
Lots of shampoo,
hear her calling.

"Lots of treasures
still with me.
But Mr Crab
is in the sea."

Roar loves stories,
lots of words.
Facts and pictures
about birds.

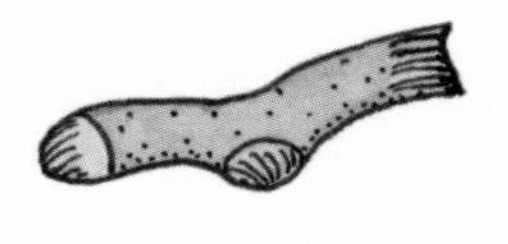

"Blackbirds, ravens,
magpies, crows.
Who's that sitting
on my toes?"
Birds.

Roar likes bed-time,
time to talk.
Telling Daddy
of her walk.

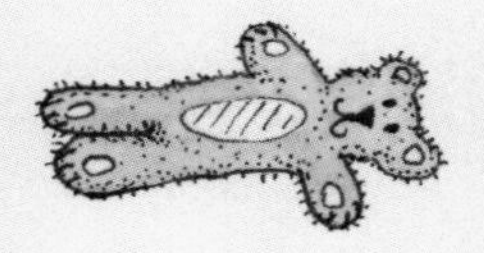

"Goodnight, Daddy,
go downstairs.
Birds have feathers,
dogs have hairs."

Daddy peers
around the door.
Sings a song
for little Roar.

"You search and find,
collect and store.
I love the way
that you explore.

You are a clever
dinosaur.
I celebrate
my little Roar."

"What's next?"

Other Roar books available from LDA are:

Hello, Roar, Little Dinosaur (*intended to introduce Roar to children*)
Roar's Creating, Let's Get Making!
Roar's In Shorts, Let's Play Sports!
Roar's Strumming, Let's Get Humming!
Roar's About, Let's Go Out!

Come on, Roar, Let's Explore!
ISBN: 978-1-85503-555-3

First published 2012
Printed in the UK for LDA

LDA, Findel Education, Hyde Buildings, Ashton Road, Hyde, Cheshire, SK14 4SH